First edition 2015

Library of Congress Catalog Card Number 2013953399
ISBN 978-0-7636-7280-5 (hardcover)
ISBN 978-0-7636-6885-3 (paperback)

14 15 16 17 18 19 TLF 10 9 8 7 6 5 4 3 2 1
Printed in Dongguan, Guangdong, China

This book was typeset in Frutiger and Cafeteria.
The illustrations were created digitally.

Candlewick Entertainment
An imprint of Candlewick Press
99 Dover Street
Somerville, Massachusetts 02144

visit us at www.candlewick.com

NELLY NITPICK,
KID CRITIC

CANDLEWICK
ENTERTAINMENT

FIZZY'S LUNCH LAB

Where Laughter Is Our Favorite Ingredient

PROFESSOR FIZZY
Our Host and Hero

MIXIE BOT
Best. Kitchen. Gadget. Ever.

AVRIL AND HENRY
Best Friends and Fizzy's Helping Hands

FREEZER BURN
Rock 'n' Roll Reinforcements

CORPORAL CUP
Recipe Toughie

SULLY THE CELL
Our Guide to the Human Body

NELLY NITPICK
Picky Eater and Host of the
Television Show *The Finicky Fork*

Greetings, Lunch Labbers!

I'm Professor Fizzy, and I just *love* food TV shows. I even have one of my own—I'm the host of *Lunch Lab Live!* But today I'm checking out the competition.

Welcome back to *The Finicky Fork.* I'm your host, Nelly Nitpick. Now, they say I'm this town's pickiest food critic. But I say I just know what I like: something tasty!

Professor Fizzy, what are you watching?

Oh, I know her. She's that food critic who gives a bad review to anyone who serves vegetables. Nobody knows what she looks like!

Let's get to this week's review, shall we? I went to Mike's Hot Dish and got the tuna fish. Great! Then I tried the casserole. Vegetables! Eww! Mike, you get an F from the Finicky Fork!

She is one tough cookie!

She sure is.

Don't go anywhere, because after these messages, I'll reveal where the Finicky Fork will be digging in next!

Veggie Rock

Veggies are **AMAZING,** and if you want, you can have some.

WINTER SQUASH and **SUMMER SQUASH**
are good in spring and autumn.

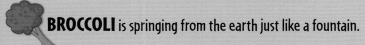**BROCCOLI** is springing from the earth just like a fountain.

Veggies come from **EVERYWHERE—**
the dirt, the sea, the mountains.

Veggies can be lots of **FUN,** veggies are **DELECTABLE,**

So become a food champion and have yourself a **VEGETABLE.**

Have yourself a **PEPPER**—eat it raw or you could grill it.

Have yourself a **PUMPKIN** or a **BEET** or have a **CARROT.**

Have yourself a **PEA** or two, or maybe five or ten.

Despair not; it's **ASPARAGUS** and it's sent from heaven!

Veggies can be lots of **FUN,** veggies are **DELECTABLE,**

So become a food champion
and have yourself a **VEGETABLE!**

I don't know about you, kids, but Freezer Burn always makes me hungry! Those vegetables truly sounded delicious. If you ask me, that Nelly Nitpick doesn't know what she's missing.

As promised, I'm on the hunt again. And this time, I'll be visiting the only place in town I haven't reviewed yet: Professor Fizzy's Lunch Lab!

But I thought you said that fries are full of bad fat!

That's true, Henry. And certain kinds of fats can cause a serious traffic jam in your arteries. Sully, can you explain?

Food Fact

Fat helps your body to build cells, create energy, and absorb vitamins.

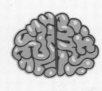

9

"Sure thing, Professor Fizzy!"

Traffic on the Arteries

"I've got Pat, an essential good fat, on board, and we're on our way to the brain, which needs healthy fats to function properly."

"It's true! And I'm in all kinds of tasty things— like fish, nuts, and— uh-oh, watch out!"

"Who's this clown? He's taking up the whole artery! Buddy, could you move, please?"

"Uh . . . no!"

"I don't think I like this guy, Pat!"

"Well, Sully, there's no reason you should. He's a trans fat. His kind of fat is bad for your body because it clogs up your arteries. It's found in fried foods—French fries, fried chicken—and in processed foods, such as chips and candy bars."

"Jeez! Pat, we gotta get this guy out of the way! Move it, pal!"

Greasy French fries sound like something Fast Food Freddy would serve at Greasy World! Why are you making them for Nelly Nitpick?

Oh, I may just have a trick up my sleeve, kids! Stand by. You're up, Corporal Cup!

Reporting for duty, sir!

Sweet-Potato Rounds

VEGETARIAN	TIME	DIFFICULTY	SERVES
YES	About one hour	Medium	

ATTENTION, KIDS:
Always cook with a grown-up!

YOU WILL NEED

Parchment paper

 Nonstick cooking spray

 3 medium sweet potatoes, peeled and cut into 1/2-inch rounds

 1 1/2 cups panko bread crumbs

2 tablespoons olive oil

 3 tablespoons maple syrup

 1 1/2 teaspoons chili powder

 1 teaspoon kosher salt

 1/2 teaspoon black pepper

DIRECTIONS

STEP 1: Preheat the oven to 400 degrees. Line a rimmed baking sheet with parchment paper, and spray it with nonstick cooking spray.

 **STEP 2:** Place the sweet-potato rounds in a large microwave-safe bowl, and cover the bowl with a large microwave-safe plate. Microwave on high until the potatoes are just tender, 5 to 9 minutes, turning the potatoes halfway through cooking. Cool, covered, for 10 minutes, then drain potatoes in a colander.

STEP 3: Pour the bread crumbs into a shallow baking dish, and mix in the oil.

STEP 4: Toss the sweet potatoes with the maple syrup, chili powder, salt, and pepper.

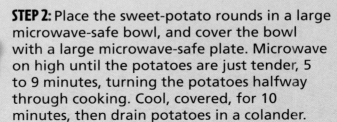 **STEP 5:** Dip each sweet-potato round into the bread crumbs and press lightly. Place the sweet-potato rounds on the prepared baking sheet, and bake until crisp, about 20 minutes.

I don't know, Professor— that Nelly Nitpick seems pretty harsh.

Oh, I'm sure she's nice—once you get to know her. And the good news is that I'll get to try out my new invention—the Perfect Patty Stamper! I just pull this lever, and it'll crank right up. . . .

Is that a burger?

CRASH! THUD!

It sure is—sort of. . . . But there's the doorbell—no time to explain!

DING-DONG!

Never mind that. On to the food! I'd like to have your best dish, please. Of course, I'll be the judge of that! Before we start, I have a few rules:

Number one: The food should be tasty!

Number two: No yucky vegetables!

Number three: You can't fool me.

This is . . . It's . . . It's GOOD! This is better than good. It's the best burger I've ever eaten. And these are the tastiest fries! Professor, you have passed the Finicky Fork test. This is the best hamburger in town!

Well, thank you, I'm glad to hear it. But that's not a hamburger.

It's not a hamburger? Then what is it?

It's a black-bean burger. It's made from black beans and veggies. And those are sweet-potato fries.

Did you say beans? Veggies? And something about sweet potatoes?

That's right! Let me show you. Henry, pass Ms. Nitpick the Lunch Lab goggles, please!

Fizzy's Goggle Inspection

Take a look at this bean burger! It's filled with all kinds of great veggies: carrots, red onions, spinach. See all these colors? It's like you're giving your body a rainbow's worth of stuff it needs—vitamins and protein.

Now, look at this hamburger from Greasy World, Ms. Nitpick. What do you think?

THE NEXT DAY . . .

The black-bean burger from Fizzy's Lunch Lab gets the highest review in *Finicky Fork* history: the coveted Golden Fork. I'm heading over there again—for the recipe!

Did you hear that, Mixie? We did it! Corporal Cup! It looks like Nelly's ready to become an honorary Lunch Labber. Can you help?

Corporal Cup's
FOOD CAMP

Ready and waiting, Professor! We'll whip Nelly into shape in no time.

Black-Bean Burger

VEGETARIAN	TIME	DIFFICULTY	SERVES
YES	Less than one hour	Hard	

ATTENTION, KIDS:
Always cook with a grown-up!

YOU WILL NEED

 Two 16-ounce cans black beans, drained and rinsed

 1/2 cup panko bread crumbs

 2 large eggs, lightly beaten

 2 scallions, minced

 1 small red onion, peeled and chopped

 1/2 cup spinach, chopped

 1/2 cup grated carrots

 3 tablespoons chopped cilantro

 2 garlic cloves, minced

 1 teaspoon ground cumin

 1/2 teaspoon dried oregano

 1 teaspoon kosher salt

 1/2 teaspoon black pepper

 1 tablespoon olive oil

DIRECTIONS

These burgers can be served with any of the following: lettuce, tomato, guacamole, salsa, Jack cheese, lime wedges, plain yogurt, or sour cream.

 **STEP 1:** Place 2 cups of the black beans in the bowl of a food processor, and pulse until chunky.

STEP 2: Transfer the processed beans to a large mixing bowl, and add the whole black beans, bread crumbs, eggs, scallions, red onion, spinach, carrots, cilantro, garlic, cumin, and oregano, and mix until well combined.

 **STEP 3:** Divide the mixture into 4 patties, about an inch thick. Sprinkle them with the salt and pepper.

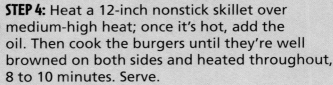 **STEP 4:** Heat a 12-inch nonstick skillet over medium-high heat; once it's hot, add the oil. Then cook the burgers until they're well browned on both sides and heated throughout, 8 to 10 minutes. Serve.

Great work whipping vegetables into shape today, Lunch Labbers! And look, here's Freezer Burn again!

Veggies can be lots of **FUN,** veggies are **DELECTABLE . . .**

Corporal Cup's FOOD CAMP

Bonus Veggie Goodness

Corporal Cup reporting for duty, along with my newest recruit, Nelly Nitpick! Our mission: to share great vegetable-based recipes. Here they are!

ATTENTION, KIDS:

Always cook with a grown-up!

Corporal Cup's
FOOD CAMP

I don't know, but I've been told:
carrots and dip are best served cold!

Baby Carrots
and Confetti Dip

VEGETARIAN	TIME	DIFFICULTY	SERVES
V	🕐	**E**	**4**
YES	Less than 30 minutes	Easy	

YOU WILL NEED

 1/2 cup shredded carrots

 1/2 cup shredded English cucumber*

 **1/2 cup** whole milk Greek yogurt*

 1/4 teaspoon minced or pressed garlic

 Pinch kosher salt

 28 baby carrots

DIRECTIONS

STEP 1: Whisk shredded carrots, cucumber, yogurt, garlic, and salt together in a medium bowl until combined.

STEP 2: Serve immediately with the baby carrots, or cover and refrigerate for up to 1 day.

*FIZZY'S TIPS: If you can't find Greek yogurt, place 1 cup of whole or low-fat regular yogurt in a strainer or colander lined with muslin or a paper towel, and set the colander over a bowl. Refrigerate for two hours and discard the liquid in the bowl. If using a regular cucumber, remove the seeds before shredding.

Cheese, garlic, AND broccoli? How can we go wrong?

Broccoli Pesto

VEGETARIAN	TIME	DIFFICULTY	SERVES
V		M	4
YES	About 30 minutes	Medium	

YOU WILL NEED

 1/2 head broccoli florets, stems removed

 2 garlic cloves, thinly sliced

 **1 1/4 cups** coarsely chopped fresh basil leaves

 1/3 cup olive oil

 1/4 cup grated Parmesan cheese

 Pinch salt

DIRECTIONS

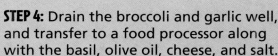

STEP 1: Fill a large bowl with ice water. Bring a large pot of water to boil.

STEP 2: Add the broccoli and garlic and boil until just tender, about 10 minutes.

STEP 3: Drain the broccoli and garlic and transfer to the bowl of ice water to stop the cooking; let it sit until completely cooled, about 5 minutes.

STEP 4: Drain the broccoli and garlic well, and transfer to a food processor along with the basil, olive oil, cheese, and salt.

STEP 5: Process until smooth, and serve over pasta.

Food Fact

You should try to eat two cups of fruit and two cups of vegetables per day.

Just delicious vegetables, cadets—no mashing around! (Well, maybe a little.)

Cauliflower Mash

VEGETARIAN	TIME	DIFFICULTY	SERVES
YES	About 30 minutes	Medium	

YOU WILL NEED

 1 head cauliflower, florets and stem cut into small chunks

 1 tablespoon unsalted butter

 1 small russet potato, peeled and diced

 Kosher salt and black pepper to taste

DIRECTIONS

 **STEP 1:** Place the cauliflower, potato, and water in a medium saucepan, and bring to a boil over high heat.

STEP 2: Lower the heat to a simmer, cover, and steam until the cauliflower and potato are tender, about 20 minutes.

 **STEP 3:** Using a slotted spoon, transfer the vegetables to a food processor. Reserve some cooking water.

 **STEP 4:** Add the butter and process until smooth, adding the cooking water as needed to allow the machine to do its work.

STEP 5: Season with salt and pepper to taste. Serve.

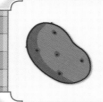 **Food Fact**

The potato was the first vegetable to be grown in space!

Corporal Cup's
FOOD CAMP

Prepare to feel cozy!
That's an order!

Roasted Squash Soup

VEGETARIAN	TIME	DIFFICULTY	SERVES
V	🕐	**M**	**6**
NO	More than one hour	Medium	

YOU WILL NEED

1 medium butternut squash, peeled, seeded, and cut into 1 1/2-inch chunks

3 tablespoons olive oil

1 large onion, peeled and chopped

Kosher salt and black pepper

1 quart low-sodium chicken broth

2 sprigs thyme

1/2 cup low-fat sour cream

DIRECTIONS

STEP 1: Preheat the oven to 400 degrees. Toss the squash with two tablespoons of the oil and spread out on a rimmed baking sheet. Roast, stirring occasionally, until the squash cubes can be easily pierced with a fork, about 45 minutes.

STEP 2: While the squash cubes are roasting, heat a large saucepan over medium-low heat; once hot, add the oil. Add the onion, 1 1/2 teaspoons salt, and 1/4 teaspoon pepper. Cook about 20 minutes. Add the chicken broth, thyme, and roasted squash cubes to the pot and bring to a simmer. Cook for 10 minutes.

STEP 3: Remove the thyme and carefully purée the soup in small batches in a blender until smooth. Stir in the sour cream. Serve.

FIZZY'S TIPS: Make a vegetarian version of this soup by substituting vegetable stock for the chicken broth. Peeled and seeded butternut squash can be found in the refrigerated section of your supermarket's produce aisle.

This veggie stir-fry has made a true recruit out of me!

Stir-Fry with Mushrooms

VEGETARIAN	TIME	DIFFICULTY	SERVES
V	**L**	**H**	**4**
YES	Less than one hour	Hard	

YOU WILL NEED

 1 cup cold water

 2 tablespoons low-sodium soy sauce

 1 tablespoon cornstarch

 1 tablespoon rice vinegar

 1/2 teaspoon toasted sesame oil

 1/2 teaspoon Asian chili paste (optional)

 1 tablespoon peanut oil

 4 cups bite-size broccoli florets (about 1/2 head)

 1 red bell pepper, sliced thin

 12 button mushrooms, halved if small or sliced if large

 1 tablespoon chopped fresh ginger root

 2 garlic cloves, chopped

 1 small head coarsely chopped bok choy (about **2 cups** chopped)

 1 cup snow peas, trimmed

 1 bunch scallions, root and 1 inch of green part trimmed and discarded, remainder cut diagonally into 1-inch pieces

 1/2 cup bean sprouts

DIRECTIONS

STEP 1: Whisk the water, soy sauce, cornstarch, rice vinegar, sesame oil, and chili paste (if using) together in a small bowl, and set aside.

STEP 2: Heat a large nonstick skillet or a wok over high heat. When the pan is smoking hot, carefully add the peanut oil. Add the broccoli, bell pepper, and mushrooms, and cook until the broccoli is bright green, 2–4 minutes. Push the vegetables aside to make a clearing in the center of the pan. Add the ginger and garlic and cook until just golden, about 1 minute. Stir in the bok choy and snow peas and cook until they are bright green but still retain some of their crunch, about 2 minutes.

STEP 3: Stir the reserved soy sauce mixture to recombine, then pour into the skillet, and bring to a boil. Add the scallions and bean sprouts, and cook for one minute longer. Serve immediately.

At ease, cadets! This soup spells it out for you—D-E-L-I-C-I-O-U-S!

Veggie Alphabet Soup

VEGETARIAN	TIME	DIFFICULTY	SERVES
V	L	M	6
NO	About 30 minutes	Medium	

YOU WILL NEED

 1 tablespoon olive oil

  2 carrots, peeled and sliced thin

 1 medium onion, peeled and chopped fine

 1 celery rib, sliced thin

8 cups low-sodium chicken broth

1 large tomato, seeds removed and chopped into 1/2-inch pieces

 2 sprigs thyme

 1 small yellow summer squash, chopped into 1/2-inch pieces

 1 cup green beans, trimmed and cut into 1/2-inch pieces

 6 ounces small alphabet pasta

 2 tablespoons chopped parsley

 Salt and pepper

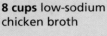

DIRECTIONS

STEP 1: Heat the olive oil in a large pot over medium-high heat. When hot, add the carrots, onion, and celery, and cook until lightly browned, about 5 minutes. Stir in the broth, tomato, and thyme, and bring to boil. Reduce the heat to medium-low and simmer, covered, until the vegetables are just tender, about 10 minutes.

STEP 2: Add the summer squash, green beans, and pasta, and cook until the vegetables and pasta are tender, about 6 minutes. Remove the thyme sprigs, add the parsley, and season with salt and pepper to taste. Serve.

FIZZY'S TIPS: Make a vegetarian version of this soup by substituting vegetable stock for the chicken broth. Serve with a sprinkling of Parmesan cheese for extra flavor.

This is one impressive dish, Corporal Cup! We may need reinforcements!

Very Veggie Frittata

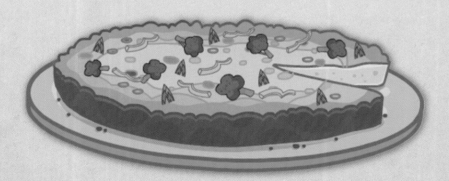

VEGETARIAN	TIME	DIFFICULTY	SERVES
V		**H**	**6**
YES	Less than one hour	Hard	

YOU WILL NEED

 8 large eggs

 1 teaspoon kosher salt

 1/2 teaspoon black pepper

 **4** scallions, finely chopped

 **2 1/2 cups** finely chopped broccoli

 1/2 cup shredded cheddar cheese, about **2 ounces**

 1/2 cup cubed cooked potatoes

 1/4 cup chopped fresh basil

 2 teaspoons olive oil

DIRECTIONS

STEP 1: With the rack in the middle position, preheat the oven to 350 degrees. Whisk the eggs, salt, and pepper together in a medium bowl. Stir in the vegetables and basil.

STEP 2: Heat a 12-inch ovenproof nonstick skillet over medium heat; once hot, add the oil. Add the egg mixture and cook, without stirring, for 1 minute. Transfer to the oven and bake until the eggs are set and the top is golden, 15–20 minutes. Turn the frittata out onto a serving plate, cut into wedges, and serve.

Food Fact

A hard-boiled egg will spin, but a soft-cooked or raw egg won't.

Corporal Cup's
FOOD CAMP

These veggies are sure to get your taste buds sizzling, cadets!

Super Veggie Sauté

VEGETARIAN	TIME	DIFFICULTY	SERVES
V		**M**	**4**
YES	About 30 minutes	Medium	

YOU WILL NEED

 1 tablespoon olive oil

 1/2 medium red onion, peeled and chopped

 2 garlic cloves, minced

 1 large zucchini, cut into 1/2-inch chunks

 3 ears of corn, kernels cut off and reserved, cobs discarded

 1 beefsteak tomato, cored and diced

 1/4 teaspoon kosher salt

 2 tablespoons chopped fresh basil leaves

DIRECTIONS

Step 1: Heat the oil in a large skillet over high heat. Add the onion and garlic, and cook, stirring occasionally, until the onion starts to lose its red color and just begins to brown, about 5 minutes.

Step 2: Add the zucchini, and cook until tender and just beginning to brown, about 12 minutes.

Step 3: Add the corn kernels, tomato, and salt, and cook, stirring frequently, until heated through, about 5 minutes.

Step 4: Stir in the basil, and serve immediately.

Food Fact

A meal should be full of color! The more color on your plate, the more variety it has and the healthier it is.